To: T
Go

Patricia Forsyth

MW00763682

THE LIFE
OF THE
OHIO COUNTY
DOG WARDENS

PATRICIA FORSYTH

authorHOUSE®

AuthorHouse™
1663 Liberty Drive
Bloomington, IN 47403
www.authorhouse.com
Phone: 1 (800) 839-8640

Published by AuthorHouse 07/15/2019

ISBN: 978-1-7283-1184-5 (sc)
ISBN: 978-1-7283-1183-8 (e)

PREFACE

The Life of the Ohio County Dog Wardens

Your job as a Dog Warden is probably one of the most unappreciated jobs in any County, of any state, in this Union. But, I'm here to tell you that you have one of the <u>most important</u> jobs in this country. Most of these jobs don't pay very well, but it is a very rewarding career.

Every call is someone complaining. If there wasn't a problem, your office phone wouldn't be ringing. Most every call that goes into the Dog Warden's Office is from a person that is upset about a dog in the neighborhood. Dogs that are wetting on their shrubs, messing in their yard, chasing their kids or killing livestock. I never thought before I became a Deputy Dog Warden that dogs could get into so much trouble.

If this country didn't have us the public couldn't walk out their door. I can't express in this book how important your job is to the public.

According to the Humane Society of the United States, one female dog and her offspring can be the source of 67,000 puppies in just 6 years. This is just one female dog. Think of the thousands of puppies that are born every day in this country. There are not enough homes for these unwanted animals. Spay and neuter is the only answer. I will touch on this farther back in this book.

FOREWORD

Dogs! There are dogs everywhere. Dog that have jobs, dogs that are pests, dogs tied in yards, dog running at large. Some dogs have even gone to war.

Dogs can breed at a fantastic rate when not controlled. There are people that are professional breeders that try to improve the breed that they have chosen to love and cherish. They show their dogs and try to get them into good homes.

Then there are the back yard breeders that are just breeding to make a quick buck. They don't care about temperament, quality, or even how they are caring for their dogs. It's just the money. There are, also, dogs that are out there not spayed or neutered and just happen to breed.

There is a new trend these days. Dogs that are deliberately mixed bred and are sold at big prices. These types of mixes can be found at any County Pound at much cheaper prices. People are fooled into thinking they just purchased a new breed or something. At the prices they are getting for these puppies a person could get a decent pure bred with papers.

Dogs can be used to guard illegal drugs or as drug sniffing dogs for police or border control. Dogs herd sheep, cattle or even ducks. Some dogs are placed with sheep to control coyote attacks. Some dogs race, some pull carts and some do obedience work.

All in all, dogs are everywhere and most times there are too many dogs and not enough homes. This is where Dog Wardens and Animal Control come in to play. Humane Societies and Societies for the Protection of Animals, also, have their place in the community. Their job is to protect animals from abuse and the Dog Warden and Animal Control's job is to protect people from stray dogs and animals.

Dog Wardens and Animal Control officers are hated by some and loved by others, but their job is very important to any community. There are funny stories, sad stories, great rescue stories and some tragic stories.

I hope to fill this book with all of the above. I want to cover every type of situation that I and other Dog Wardens have encountered. Hopefully you will learn some things, laugh a little, applaud for great rescues and maybe shed a few tears for the tragic stories of some of the dogs.

KANSAS RABBITS

Went to a small place about an acre or two on a county road where Sam Kille had fenced off about ½ acre with chicken wire. He had ordered some wild Jack rabbits from Kansas and wanted to raise them to release for hunting. The home was a nice ranch style and the area was well keep.

Something had killed these rabbits, but we didn't catch any dogs in our dog trap. Ohio law states, "any owner of horses, sheep, cattle, swine, mules, goats, domestic rabbits or domestic fowl or poultry that have an aggregate fair market value of ten dollars or more and that have been injured or killed by a dog not belonging to the owner or harbored on his premises, in order to be eligible to receive compensation from the dog and kennel fund."

We continued to try to catch any stray dogs for a couple of weeks. Mr. Kille owned several beagle dogs that he used for hunting. It may have been one of his own hunting dogs that got loose that could have killed the rabbits. It wasn't an issue for us because we weren't paying for those rabbits, they were wild.

PIGS WITH HIVES

Our office received a call from a farmer, Ted Homan, that there had been dogs in his pigs. Ted was a middle aged farmer and had two brothers that were also farmers in the same area. Ted was I think the youngest of the three. He was of medium build and had a very nice farm and buildings. Everything around his farm was neat without junk laying around. He had a large garage where he fixed his tractors in the winter.

The Dog Warden, and I went out to his farm. It was the middle of winter and the wind was awful that day. I pulled on my snowsuit and my winter cap over my ears. As we entered the barn there were about 35 pink pigs with gashes and bite marks on several of them. The pigs were so upset they had broken out in hives. Ted told us they weren't eating right and they probably would take time for them to settle down.

Ted said he had seen the dogs back on the farm when he came out of the house. We went back to the truck and got a box trap off the tailgate. We always took a trap for dogs on an animal claim whether it was sheep, cows, rabbits or whatever animal had been killed. We put dry dog food in the back of the trap on the trip board, but ask the farmer to add meat scraps to the dog food after they had supper.

We instructed him to confine his little dog so as not to catch him in the trap. His dog was a mixed black rat terrier type about 10#. He wasn't going to detour any dog from attacking the pigs. Ted told us he couldn't even hear him bark when he was in the house.

We worked on that claim in conjunction with a claim around the corner at his father's farm. On his father's farm, a brother Hank had sheep. Hank had dogs getting into his sheep. So we set a dog trap and had Hank add scraps to that trap as well.

Across the road from Dad's farm was another brother Chuck. Chuck and Ted didn't get along. Down the road was a large farm house that was rented by a farm hand to a neighboring farm.

I was just a new deputy and only been on the job for a month or so. I checked the traps daily and worked the area hard looking for loose dogs. Well boom we got another hit on Chuck's sheep. Our Kennel Master said after my frustration at not finding any dogs doing the damage, "You might want to check the big farm house down the road. They had a large German Shepherd that killed their own pig a few months back." That afternoon I went to the farm house and talked to the young woman there. Their names were Jean and Jack Thompson. The shepherd was tied by the house and I explained to her about not letting her dog loose. She was friendly and said she'd keep him tied.

About a week went by and Ted called and said his pigs had been hit again, but this time he'd seen the dogs and had his gun with him. He shot 2 of the dogs, a white shepherd, black and tan German Shepherd and the third had gotten away. He recognized the 3ed dog, it belonged to his brother Chuck.

Jack and I rushed out to his farm. We found that the Thompson's shepherd had been left loose that night and went across the road and picked up the white Shepherd that belonged to Sam White. Sam was a big good looking guy and had a very nice farm and a very good boat business. The two shepherds continued down the road and picked up Chuck's dog that just happened to be loose that night. We surmised that the Thompson's dog was the instigator because he had already had the thrill of killing a pig at his own place a few months before and the other two dogs followed. When dogs gang up and run in packs they aren't always the same sweet dogs you have around a farm.

It's like nice teenage boys that get together and then they become braver and get in trouble.

I don't think this matter made Chuck and Ted any closer because any dogs that are caught in livestock the owners have to pay the claim. The earlier claims were paid for out of our Dog and Kennel fund as per Ohio Revised Code.

The real nice thing about this story was that the white shepherd had on tags so we knew where he belonged. To prove that the other shepherd belonged to the Thompson's the Dog Warden said, "let's load up this dog and start around the block and see if we can get the owner of this shepherd to identify it himself." We headed to the farm Mr. Thompson worked on. As we drove up here comes Mr. Thompson out of the barn. When Mr. Thompson came up to the truck we got out and started shooting the breeze with him. After a while Dog Warden says to him, "We've got a dog on the truck and we're trying to find it's owner, will you give a look?" Mr. Thompson walks to the back of the truck and says, "Why hell, thanks a lot, that's my dog." We got one of the owners to pay their share of the claim which was over $3000. That was the owner of the white shepherd. The Thompson's had no money and it wasn't worth the effort to sue. Chuck's dog that Ted had identified as his brother's dog, we really had no solid proof it was his since it wasn't shot along with the other dogs and we couldn't take it to him. We didn't want the brothers feud to get any worse, the Dog Warden decide to pay the rest of the claim out of the Dog & Kennel Fund.

Believe me we protected the dog and kennel fund from people trying to fake claims, but sometimes you had to pay out even when you knew the truth, but could never prove it in a court of law.

MAYBE MY DOG DID

Now, Ted Homan's brother Chuck was still having trouble with his sheep getting killed. We had a trap still on that farm and I was going crazy trying to figure out where this other dog was coming from. When the office phone rang on that Wednesday, it was Chuck Homan. "We got a dog in the trap," he stated. I jumped up and headed out.

We had set the trap in the tractor path that goes past the sheep and down along his fields. It was still very cold and icy. When I got to the farm, Chuck was not there. This dog was a big mixed breed and not very friendly. I looked the situation over and decided with the ice I better call the Dog Warden for help. I didn't want to lose this dog.

I went back to the truck and radioed the Dog Warden for backup. In about 20 minutes he arrived and after I noosed the dog the Dog Warden added another noose. It was a good thing he did. We were slipping and sliding and the dog was definitely trying to get away.

When we got him back to the kennel and unloaded, he went back to the corner of his kennel run and never came forward. Most dogs are happy to see people and come up to the front of the kennel run. Not this dog he didn't like any of this stuff.

After a couple of days, we got a call from a man looking for his dog and this dog matched the dog he was missing. Sam Arnold lived about 1 ½ miles from Chuck's farm.

Mr. Arnold sent his wife to get the dog. She paid her poundage and we took her back into the kennel to retriever her dog. It wouldn't come out for her. We stood there about 5-6 minutes to let her coerce her dog out of the kennel. He wouldn't move from the back of the kennel run. We finely had to go back to the office and let her deal with him. Mr. Arnold was not very happy that we had picked up HIS dog. He was a retired Air Force Captain and was certain his dog wouldn't kill anything.

About a week later Chuck's sheep got hit again. Soon after that hit we had no more trouble. But Ted Homan told us later that Mr. Arnold heard about the last hit on Chuck's sheep and his dog had been loose. He shot his own dog and that ended our problems with the sheep kills in that area. Unfortunately both farmers gave up raising sheep. Their farms were to close to urbanization.

YOU CAN'T GET ME IF YOU CAN'T SEE ME

Many farmers keep sheep on the back of their farms in pastures that are to rocky to farm or do much of anything else with. When we got the call for an animal claim on Elmer Smith's farm we had several sheep down. The area was on a farm that had a beautiful creek running through it and was about 20 acres of good grass. Mr. Smith said he kept the sheep just to keep this pasture down. He didn't have a big flock. Only about 10-12 sheep. Unfortunately, he lost about half his flock on this day. A couple of the sheep only had the wool pulled out on their backs, but were dying. A couple were lying by the creek with their heads under water. After we examined them, we couldn't find a bite mark anywhere on them.

These couple of sheep being chased or scared when the other sheep were being chased had stuck their head under water to hide from the dogs and drowned.

Under Ohio law any damage that dogs cause to livestock are covered under the law because the dogs worried the sheep so much that they tried to hide by putting their head under the water in the creek.

THE NEIGHBORHOOD GANG

Dogs seem to run more in the winter. After studying this, I began to realize why dogs seemed to run more in the fall and winter. When the crops are growing the dogs can't see very far on their farms, so they don't run as much. As soon as the crops come off in the fall and during the winter we usually had more animal claims.

As usual we received a call to a farm for dogs in sheep on a very cold and icy day. When I entered the small pasture by the barn I hit the ice and down I went. I picked myself up as dignified as I could and continued toward the barn. The Dog Warden and I met the farmer, Smokey Jones and entered the barn where he keep his sheep during winter. As we were looking over the sheep the Dog Warden stepped to the door and looked down the tractor path between Smokey's fields. He said, "here come the dogs now!" Mr. Jones and I climbed to a higher part of the barn and the Dog Warden went to the truck to get his shotgun.

The 5 dogs came running into the barn and went directly to chasing the sheep. That didn't last any longer than 3 seconds. They spotted Smokey and me and out of the barn they ran right back down the tractor path that they had come on. We had gotten a good look at the dogs so we knew we'd be able to find where they lived. We ran and jumped into our two trucks and headed down the road.

As the dogs ran past the first house they dropped off the first dog. This continued right down the road. Each house they dropped off another dog. At the fifth house was a man that had a lot of hounds, but this was his wife's house dog. This again was just like a bunch of teenage boys looking for fun.

One dog alone might not get into too much, but when they pack up is when the trouble begins. It seems to stem back to the wolf instinct when they hunt in packs.

3 TOES

My call to this farm was on the strange side. The house was a huge Victorian brick house in mediocre shape. The farm owner lived down the road in a nice split level house. Toys all over the yard and about 4 little ones running around. He had about a 450# steer with it's side chewed out down at the farm. This calf was still standing but was going to have to be put down. The side of this steer had about a 12" x 8" hunk of skin ripped out of it. As I talked to the owner his dog came running up and I noticed he was probably part Husky. He had 2 toes missing on his right hind foot. I said to him, "gee, what happened to your dogs back foot?" He said, "I ran over it with my tractor." I said, "that must have hurt."

I investigated the claim, set a trap, and never caught a dog on his farm. I was suspicious of his dog, but had no firm proof that his own dog had attacked his steer. I paid the claim because I was sure it was a dog that had attacked his steer.

I received a call about three weeks later for a stray over on a road about 1 ½ miles east of Three Toes farm. When I arrived I talked to the complainant for a while and got the dog on my come-a-long. When I got the dog on the tailgate of my truck I seen he had 3 toes. Then I recognized the dog. It was Three Toes from my steer claim a few week before.

When I got back to the office I called my farmer and he said, "Well, if he doesn't stay on the farm you might as well keep him, he isn't doing me any good. I suspect that he thought his dog had done the crime, but he didn't want to admit it. We kept the dog.

DON'T MAKE A FOOL OUT OF ME

On a call just outside of town was a beautiful farm. The house had been remodeled just a few years before. The farm had been pretty run down before. The barn had been painted and new iron pole fences had been put around the corral. The fence around the pasture had been replaced with a few sheep and three horses were roaming around.

There was one sheep down and dead. It had one large hunk of wool pulled out of it's back just above the tail. It was the only injury on it.

This was, again, soon after I started and it just didn't seem right that a dog had killed it. I returned to the office and explained to Dog Warden that there was something strange about the kill. He said, "After lunch we'll go back out and see what we could make out of it.

After lunch we returned to the farm and Dog Warden looked the situation over with me and said, "See the long, wide scraps along the bite mark? One of those horses did this. The sheep probably was grazing too close to one of the horses and it got a good hold on it and ripped the wool right out of it. Mr. Farley is a friend of mine, but he isn't going to make a fool out of me and get me to pay this claim out of the Dog & Kennel Fund," he said.

All of these animal claims are a learning experience and any Dog Warden or Deputy should get all the experience they can. Go out on any claim with other deputies or the Dog Warden. I was very lucky to get this experience when I started on the job and had a wonderful mentor.

OH GOOD GRAVY, SHE'S NAKED

I was out on calls with the Dog Warden. It was lunch time and we were headed back to the kennel when we get a call from the Sheriff's dispatcher. "You are needed in Hessville immediately." Hessville is a small village of about 500 people. We turn the truck around and rush out there.

When we arrive there, there's stands the Sheriff himself, 3 deputies, and 2 EMS personnel. When the Sheriff is out on a call you know something is serious. We jump out of the truck and approach the guys. The Dog Warden says, "What's up?" The Sheriff says, "the neighbors haven't seen Mrs. Johnson around for a couple of days and they looked in the window and seen her on the sofa but can't rouse her. When we tried to enter the house there's a dog in there that won't let us in." The Dog Warden replied, "Okay, we'll get our catch poles."

When we headed toward the house with our catch poles the Dog Warden says, "Go get him Pat." I know I thought, "thanks a heck of a lot." As I entered the house this ferocious dog starts growling and charging me. My loop is open and as I'm trying to get it over his head it scares him and he runs to another room. I take a quick look at the sofa and good god the woman is naked and has one leg up on the back of the sofa. She has a towel across her belly, but it isn't covering anything important. I'm thinking, "Oh great and I'm the only woman there." Well, back to chasing the dog so the Sheriff and EMS personnel can get in the house. The dog gets so scared that he runs upstairs so I shut the stairway door. At least he's confined. I then go to the front door and tell the guys, "You can come in now the dog's confined. As the Dog Warden comes in he takes a glance at the sofa and says, "We better get the dog." We head up stairs and chased it around a bit, but got it cornered and took it out to the truck.

Oh something I forgot to tell you was that this dog was about 7" at the shoulder and didn't weigh probably 10#. He was one of the nastiest dog I ever seen. We held him at the shelter until we could get someone to come in to release him to us. We had him for a month and no one could get him to make up.

CRAZY CASES

WILD MAN

One of the weirdest people I ever had to deal with was Howard. He lived on a property just outside the city limits. I understood he got his land rent free in exchange for keeping up the acre of land where his trailer sat.

It was one of those small old trailers from the late '40s or early '50s. It was leaf green and about 18-20 feet long.

Howard ran around in Bermuda type shorts, no shirt, dark hair that stuck up and he was as skinny as a rail. He went barefoot usually in the summer and had large sores on the inside of both ankles. He was a scary sight to say the least.

He would call because his neighbors would let their dogs loose and they would mess in the yard. Our office girl, Cathy, thought it was very funny when I would get a call from him. I hated going out there only because he was a very scary looking person and the fact that I had found out he had shot and killed his brother years before. He had never made any bad gestures toward me, but he would rant and rave about the dogs running. I'd talk to the neighbors and tell them to keep there dogs tied because I never seen any dog loose. Then I'd go back and set a trap to keep Howard happy, although there wasn't anywhere to hide it. There weren't any other building to set it behind, just open land. Anyone could see it there, so the dogs wouldn't run until I'd pick up the trap and it would start all over in a week or two.

This went on for a couple of years. The next to the final call at his place was a call Cathy received from Howard that he needed dog licenses for his two dogs and he had no way to get in to purchase them. When I arrived back at the office after a previous call there stood Cathy with a big grin on her face. "Guess who wants to see you?" she said with a smart aleck sort of smile. I just looked at her and she said, "Howard". I made a face and said, "Now what?" He needed dog licenses and couldn't get in to town.

I had never been in his small trailer before and I wasn't happy when he invited me to come in. We usually didn't enter a persons home, but the way he was dressed and it was January I stepped into the trailer. He had two very friendly dogs. One was a lab mix and the other was a small terrier mix. Their tails were wagging as they jumped up on his couch. There was dog hair all over the couch and floor and the trailer smelled dreadful. It was the smell of the two dogs that had never had been bathed. Above the kitchen counter were three small shelves about 13-14 inches long. On the shelves were about 5 cans of food. There was nothing laying around, no clothes strewn, nothing laying on the counters. Other than the dog hair, he didn't have a mess. I sold him his tags and left.

I didn't hear from him or anything about him until late that summer. I got a call on the Sheriff's radio to get to Howard's address. I needed to pick up his dogs as he had passed away. As I approached his road, I was stopped by a Sheriff's deputy. I said to him, "He's not still in there is he?" Deputy Willey said, "No, they've already taken him out, but when he died his head went in a bucket that was sitting by the wall." I said, "I hope he's not there because I don't want to get into what you guys did to me the last time."

JIM AND THE WHITE BOXER

My Deputy, Jim, received a call from a frantic woman. Seems she went outside to get into her car and a white boxer ran at her. She had an appointment she needed to get to, but couldn't get to her car.

Jim rushed over there and when he got out of his truck he didn't see a dog anywhere. As he approached the lady's porch the dog surprised him as it ran out from under a bush. He had his come-a-long with him and pointed it at the dog. That scared the dog and it scampered around the house. The homeowner came out on her porch and started thanking Jim for getting rid of the dog. Jim said, "Madam, please go back in the house I haven't got a hold of the dog yet." Jim wandered around the house looking for the dog and it ran to the woman's porch. When Jim finally noosed the dog it jumped around like crazy and bit the come-a-long until it broke off one of it's teeth. When Jim came back to the kennel he handed me the tooth and we keep it around the office until I retired. I think I still have it here somewhere here at home. I think if I come across it I'm going to have it made into a necklace for Jim.

LIVING IN A CAVE?

It has always been easy to divide our county between 2 deputies. We have a river that runs almost in the middle of the county. It runs right through our county seat. One deputy handles the westside of the county and the other deputy handles the eastside.

The previous Dog Warden, felt that by keeping a person in the same territory that they know where the problems are and know the people. It's a bit different than a large department where you have 10 Deputies and they get bored because they have a small area to patrol. When you have 2 Deputies for a whole county they don't have much time to get bored with their area.

Along our river on the south west side of town are caves in the rock. We had a man and his dog living in one of the larger caves. We'd get complaints when he would wander around town because he would leave the dog at the cave and it would bark.

We found out that this guy was the same one that had been living in a very nice neighborhood and had been a problem there. He'd been left some money, but he was on drugs. He ended up, apparently, in the cave because he lost the house. We heard he was getting some money from a

21

trust fund handled by his brother. Whether this was true we have no idea.

People wanted us to do something about the dog. Ohio don't have a barking law. He didn't let the dog run at large, but he had no license. How do you cite a man for no license that has nothing but his dog. Don't know whatever happened to him, but it ended up as a problem for the county Sheriff.

I PINGED HIM!

This is a man I call Red. It's obvious he had red hair. He was a very nice guy and the Dog Warden and I enjoyed visiting when he had dog problems. His barns were rather run down but he milked cows and raised a few heifer calves to replace his old cows.

Red had a fairly nice house and with his parents he had several farms. Red's parents lived at the edge of our county and the farm where he lived was in the next county to the south and west by a few roads.

Red's family had antique cars in several of the barns and I mean a lot of them. They didn't fix them up or anything and we could never figure out why they acquired them and never did anything with them. But in the bottom of the raised barns they raised pigs. On Red's main farm he had milk cows.

Red wore the same bib overalls everyday. I don't mean the same kind, I mean the same ones. When we'd meet him in the barn I couldn't believe how gross everything looked. The barn was in disrepair, the standing stalls didn't look very clean and he'd be milking in his bibs covered with a months whatever. Still he was a real nice character to talk to.

We had several hits on his pigs and no dogs were ever

seen. Finally we were called to the farm where the pigs were and Red's Mom met us there. She had shot a large St. Bernard and hit it in its lung. It lay there dying, breathing hard. Red's Mom was a small framed woman and she had to be 85 years old. As she walked up to us she looked at us and exclaimed, "I pinged him." She was carrying an old 22 rifle.

The dog died quickly and we never found an owner, but Red's Mom is one of the oldtimer.

WHAT A GREASY MESS

Time to go home for supper. "It's 4:30 and what a day," I'm thinking as I get off the by-pass by the kennel. Unit 22, Sheriff, Unit 22, Sheriff. "Darn," I'm thinking as I answer to sheriff's call. "You're needed at the water treatment plant ASAP." I gave the Sheriff dispatcher a 10-4 and was on my way. Dog gone it, supper will be late for the kids again tonight.

When I arrived at the City Water Treatment Plant I was led up a back stairs to a flat roof over a shorter part of the building. There the operator for the evening showed me his problem. He was just about to start these very large motors and decided to walk out and check them first. It was a very lucky break for a white American Eskimo dog that had gotten under one of the motors and couldn't get out.

The motors were bolted to an angle iron frame and the dog had crawled over the frame at the bottom, but couldn't get out at the front as it was to small of an opening. Unfortunately, when he tried to back out over the angle iron frame he would bump against it and couldn't seem to get his legs over the frame. I noosed the dog and lifted his back legs over the frame and he backed out very easily.

The problem was this white dog was black with grease

from head to toe. I didn't think anyone would pickup this poor greasy pooch, but they did.

The man at the Treatment Plant said it's a good thing he didn't start the motors as they are very loud.

We sort of surmised that the dog may have chased a rabbit or something up the steps and it went under the motor, because the Treatment Plant is next to a park. The owner did pick up their dog and put it in their car. I sure wouldn't want to clean up that greasy dog, yet alone the car after that dog went home.

THE NUN

In our city there is a beautiful get away across the road from a small golf course. It's up a large hill and across from the river. The grounds are covered with large old pines and the large old home can't be seen from the road. It's, also, a get away for Catholic nuns. They go there for retreats and to rest and enjoy the quiet, beautiful surroundings.

On one summer day I receive a call from Sister Pauline and she is explaining to me that there are some noisey dogs across the road from the Pines that are barking all night and disturbing the peace of the visiting nuns.

I tell her we will go out and have a talk with the owner, but there isn't any Ohio law against barking dogs.

My officer drives to the area and there are several walker hounds penned there. But, there isn't a house so no one is living on the property. My officer inquires at the golf course and finds out that they are allowing a man to keep his dogs there. Well we find the owner in a village a few miles away and talk to him about the barking and that it is disturbing the nuns.

My feeling is that the dogs barked at night because the wildlife was wandering and of course the dogs wanting to get out and chase them was driving them nuts.

I received several calls in the next few weeks and with each call Sister Pauline was getting madder and madder because we couldn't seem to do anything about it.

Low and behold one day Sister Pauline shows up at my office and she was steamed. With her she had a cassette that she had taped with the barking dogs on it. I still couldn't get it through to her that my office couldn't cite the owner over barking dogs. So we played about 10 minutes of the tape and we couldn't hear one barking dog ONLY THE BEAUTIFUL SONGS OF THE BIRDS IN THE PINES.

DON'T BE SCARED GUYS

I was only on the job for a year or so when I get a week end call from the sheriff's office. There's a mean dog harassing people out on County Road 39.

I was right in the middle of baking cookies with my kids and I had flour on my t-shirt, my hair was a mess. My sister-in-law, that lived next door, was over and she wanted to go with me to pick up this dog.

Remember this was the late 1970's and I was the first female deputy dog warden to work the road.

We jumped in the Dog Warden's truck and off we go. When we arrived there was a pick up truck parked very close to the carport with 4 or 5 large men standing around concerned about this mean dog. On the carport there were a couple of bikes leaning against the house. I parked in the drive, but back aways from the parked pickup. I left my sister-in-law in the truck and went to the bed of the truck and got my come-a-long. I started up toward the guys and they started to tell me how mean this dog acted. I walked between the truck and the edge of the house which was just enough room to get through. The dog had taken refuge behind the bikes. As I approached the dog he started growling so I started quietly talking to him. He was a short,

29

stocky built bulldog type. I slowly slipped the noose over the bikes and continued to talk to him. When I got the noose over his head and tightened it he charged out from behind the bikes.

While all this was going on the guys had closed the space where I entered the carport and were trying to get out of the way. I had the dog and started for my truck through the space I had entered the carport. I said to the guys, "look out fellows" and men scattered all over the place. I took the dog to my truck, placed him in a cage, gave the guys a wave and jump in the truck. The guys stood looking at us as if they couldn't believe what they had just seen.

Always remember though that a dog will make you look great or they can make you look stupid.

DON'T ROB MY BANK

Our county Auditor (by state law) is in charge of dog licensing. Every time dog license price have gone up he said we would lose about 1500people buying dog licenses.

Those were the times we would hire personnel to go door to door and check licenses. We used our kennel worker to supervise 18 year olds to knock on doors and write tickets to persons that hadn't purchased their license.

The best thing we did was ask the Auditor if we could handle all license sales. We could get the new licenses on the computer faster than his help could. Not that they were slow, but they handle many other things in that office and dog licenses took a back seat. They handle real estate and monies paid into the county treasurer. Those things had to come first.

Fortunately our Auditor and especially his employees were glad to get some of that work off their desks.

Well, our dog license checkers were sent into a small town and came across a rather rude cop. He didn't think he should get a ticket for not purchasing a license for his dog.

I received a phone call from this unfortunate soul and got a royal chewing out for about five minutes. He then requested that I pull his ticket. When I refused he said,

"What about professional courtesy?" I said to him, "Are you going to let me go if I rob your bank?" His reply was "NO". I then replied, "Well, your robbing my bank." He hung up on me.

I have always had a problem with this cop stuff of Professional Courtsey. They let their fellow officers get away with murder. My opinion is they should follow the laws because they know better and they expect me to obey them.

CASE OF THE BAD CANDY

One of my employees, Annie, loved to play practical jokes. One of our male helpers from our welfare department, Jose, always laid his cigarettes on one of the desks before he went to clean the kennel.

Annie just couldn't help herself and if she was in the office she always picked up the pack and dumped them all over the desk. Jose never complained he just picked them up and put them back into the pack.

My very favorite prank that came back to get Annie started by her picking on the ladies at the Auditor's Office. Annie was appointed to pick up all the mail from our county complex going to the Court House mail room and the different departments in the Court House. She, also, did our pay-ins of monies that we collected at our office. When she would go to the Auditor's Office she would pull pranks on all the ladies and I hadn't heard anything about it until this big one occurred. If anyone pulled a prank on Annie she had to better them. I never found out what started this one, but I figured it must have been a good one.

Annie came in one morning with a nice one layer box of chocolate nut candy. She had opened the cellophane so well that you couldn't tell it had been opened. She opened the box and in it she had collected doggie doo and covered it with chocolate and peanuts. She slipped the cellophane back on and sealed it back up. This was around the time people were tampering with all kinds of products. I told her she better not do what she had in mind because that was product tampering, but with Annie she had a bad streak in her and she had to get the better of whoever she was trying to get.

When she delivered the mail that Friday she left the candy on the Auditor's Office counter with the mail. Well, of course, the ladies knew who had brought it in. The ladies didn't say a word about it for a about a month. Annie thought the whole thing had gone off with out a catch.

On this one Friday I get a call from Babe at the Auditors. She ask me if Annie had said anything about the box of candy. I told her I hadn't heard anything out of Annie because I had ask her the first week if the ladies had said anything.

Babe told me that all the ladies in the Auditors were going to wait until Annie delivered the mail and Janie a clerk in the back office of the Auditors was going to nonchalantly walk up to which ever lady wasn't waiting on Annie and in a low voice but loud enough for Annie to hear, tell the other clerk that the Auditor and the County Commissioners were getting sued over that box of candy because of that piece of candy that they had given that little girl that came in the office. The girls mother was furious and had filed a law suit.

Well Annie of course over heard this and left to come back to our office. Annie went on with her morning calls and she didn't say a thing. Before noon I get a call from Babe and she wants to know if Annie had said anything. I told her no and she wasn't even acting funny.

Right after lunch Annie comes in my office and tells me she's going to lose her job. I ask her why what's going on. I played along and told her she should never have done that. As soon as Annie leaves the office to take a call on a dog running at large I call Babe and tell her Annie is really upset and don't leave her hanging all weekend.

Annie had to stew all afternoon and just 5 minutes before we closed the phone rings. Annie answers as I walk out of my office. I see her holding the reviever a foot from her ear and just looking at it. I said, "What's the matter?" Annie says, "All they said was Got You." She still sat at her desk and looked puzzled. I stood there for a minute, but she still wasn't getting the phone call, so I said, "Annie, it was Babe, she was telling you she got you."

This still never stopped Annie even though for a whole day she was sure she was going to lose her job.

CAT WARDEN

By the time this happened Babe had moved out to the Election Board Office. Annie was still picking up mail at the County Complex. As always what brought this on I don't know or maybe I don't remember because I hate practical jokes.

While Annie was in the Election Board office one of the ladies slipped out the back door and taped a paper over Annie's license plate on her truck that said, "CAT WARDEN." Babe then called a police officer friend of hers and convinced him to stop her for a fictitious license plate. He was reluctant to do it but agreed. When she hit our main street in town he caught up with her and hit his police lights behind her. She pretended she didn't see him and turned off behind our local Post Office and he finally got her stopped behind there. She was very embarrassed but she never said anything to any of us in the office. We heard it from Babe.

I'm sure she had to best them again, but I never heard a thing.

NO CATS ALLOWED

We have a great guy in our community that really gives back to people. He belongs to several clubs and works the fair. He is a great photographer and has a studio and camera shop. Karl likes to feed the wild birds and has had a lot of trouble keeping the cats from his neighborhood from coming around his bird feeder and killing his wild birds he feeds.

One day he got fed up and he got out a small gun and shot a neighbors cat. A neighbor seen him and all the other side of heaven broke out. Karl was cited into court, the ASPCA screamed so loud, the local newspaper got involved and Karl got letters from all over the country. People said he was nuts and needed help. He would turn into a people killer and he was really raked over the coals.

Karl was cited into court and he was fined, but it was suspended. Karl was just a normal nice guy that got discussed with unleashed cats. He also owned a couple of dogs and I know he loved them.

Some people just have had enough and enough is enough.

SUBMISSIVE DOG

A Dog Warden that I learned a lot off of and has already passed away was Steve. He was an ex-Marine. He was short and stocky built and in some ways I thought he was a little extreme.

I heard that he made his new employees go in with a mean dog and handle it. I know for a fact that some of his employees had scars on their hands. These older Dog Wardens were characters and so much fun to talk to and listen to their stories.

One of the stories Steve told me was about this puppy that his deputies just couldn't get close enough to catch. So he went out to the area and drove around until he spotted the pup. He started to talk to the puppy as he slowly slipped out of his truck. Just like his officers stated to him, the puppy stayed just out of reach of a come-a-long. Steve followed it for awhile and then it struck him. He laid on the sidewalk on his side with his leg up in the air like a submissive dog. Sure enough the puppy started toward him to give him a whiff. When the pup got close enough he made a grab and BINGO he had the puppy.

As he was getting up from the ground with the pup in his arms and a big smile on his face he looked toward the house he was in front of. There went his smile as there was an elderly lady peeking out of the curtain and apparently seen his unusual way of dog catching.

I CAN BARK TOO!

Another one of his tales that I sincerely loved began on a snowy day. He went on a call at an abandon warehouse. The complainant stated that there were dogs living in the warehouse. When he left his truck and started walking around he started up a small incline that was very icy. Down he went and just then here comes a couple of dogs charging at him growling and barking. In a split second he jumped up on his knees and started his charge back at them growling and barking just like they did. It gave him a chance to get back to his feet as the dogs retreated a ways. He got those dogs also, but except for quick thinking he could have been mauled.

SPIDERS, YUCK

There was a lady that lived in Steve's town that was very old and very poor. Her house was run down, she wore her hair on top of her head and apparently didn't wash it much. Steve's deputies went to her house on a couple of occasions and they always reported back that her friendly pet spider was still living in her hair.

Steve decided he need to see this and made a trip to her house the next time there was a complaint. Sure enough, a spider had a web in her hair and was very happy living in it's nice web home.

KENNEL CLEANING

CLEANING AND DISINFECTING
THE DOG KENNEL RUNS

1. Move dogs into clean empty pens. If you are overloaded with to many dogs and puppies put them in the cages in your vans or pickup trucks. You can also chain them across the aisle on 6' chains until their runs are cleaned and squeegeed.

2. Remove all used food and water dishes. If a dog has food left, put it in a clean dish and set it aside for the same dog at feeding time.

3. Spray back all fecal matter with the hose. Do not scrape fecal matter first and push it into the drain in a pile. It will plug the drains. Spraying it back with water breaks it down for better flow in the sewer lines and less likely to clump and block the flow.

4. Be sure to spray down the sides of the kennel runs and the doors. Many dog jump up on the sides trying to get out. If they defecate and walk in it before it can be cleaned they will have fecal matter on the walls and chain link fence.

5. When all fecal matter and urine is removed from runs spray kennel runs and kennel run doors with a disinfectant that is safe for animals.

6. Let the disinfectant set for at least 10 minutes. While it is setting, wash your dog dishes. Wash dog dishes in detergent and a small amount of bleach to disinfect.

7. After letting disinfectant set for 10 minutes, squeegee water into kennel drain.

8. Repeat process until all kennel run are cleaned.

9. Place fresh water in each kennel and return dogs to cleaned kennel run.

10. On Fridays-use bleach instead of disinfectant. Bleach is to be left on the walls and doors for 10 minutes, but to be sprayed off because bleach can be injurious to the dogs.

*All dogs water and food dishes should be stainless steel. Plastic will hold disease and the dogs will chew them up.

* Feed dogs on your own schedule. I preferred to feed the dogs around 3:00 p.m. because they seem to want to relieve themselves as soon as they are feed.

* If you get parvo in your kennel have employees bleach on that day too.

* If you have outside dog houses do not use blankets or rugs in them. They will draw moisture during cold damp days. Use straw and cedar chips. The cedar chips keep fleas down and the straw is warm and doesn't draw moisture.

BITE STICKS

When I started as a Road Deputy with the Dog Warden Department, the Dog Warden told me to always carry a bite stick at a residence when I got out of the truck. I thought that was the goofiest thing I'd ever heard of.

It didn't take me long to figure out it was the safest thing to do. I got a call about a stray Beagle to be picked up so I headed out into the county. When I pulled into the drive at this nice farm there was a large dog tied to a tree with a rope. No beagle around. I jumped out of the truck and headed to the back door of the farm house. No one was home and since there was no dog around I left a card on the door and told the home owner that if the dog returned to let me know and I'd come back.

As I just reached my truck, I turned and seen that dog that had been tied to the tree had broke his rope and was charging me at a full run. I just made it into the truck as he bounded against the truck door. You can bet my heart was pounding and I never ever got out of my truck again without my bite stick.

There are several different types of bite sticks you can use. If you're a 1 or 2 man department and haven't much money to spend do something cheap. We carried a cut off broom stick about 30' long with a ½" hole in the top end and a piece of 3/8" x 8" rawhide tied through the hole. We used it as a walking stick and could hang it on our arm to free both hands. You could carry an asp or a regular cane.

The thing you want to <u>NOT</u> do when your getting attacked or charged by a dog is to raise the bite stick in the air to swing at the dog. While you have the bite stick in the air, the dog will have your leg.

ALWAYS KEEP THE BITE STICK POINTED AT THE DOG. The dog will keep his mind on what is in front of him and you want that to be the bite stick.

The meanest dog I ever had to deal with was a mixed black & tan little short haired terrier that had the fight of a champion prize fighter. He attacked and chewed on my bite stick as I retreated to my truck about 50' away. I was never bitten by a stray dog in my 25 ½ years as a Deputy Dog Warden and Dog Warden.

CPSIA information can be obtained
at www.ICGtesting.com
Printed in the USA
LVHW010332230819
628526LV00001B/15